On Sudden Hill

For Stephen – LS

*For Auntie Jan and summers spent
painting at Pondok – BD*

SIMON AND SCHUSTER
First published in Great Britain in 2014 by Simon and Schuster UK Ltd, 1st Floor, 222 Gray's Inn Road, London WC1X 8HB
A CBS Company • Text copyright © Linda Sarah 2014 • Illustration copyright © Benji Davies 2014 • The right of Linda Sarah
and Benji Davies to be identified as the author and illustrator of this work has been asserted by them in accordance with
the Copyright, Designs and Patents Act, 1988 • All rights reserved, including the right of reproduction in whole or in part
in any form • A CIP catalogue record for this book is available from the British Library upon request • Printed in China
ISBN: 978-1-4711-1928-6 (HB) • ISBN: 978-1-4711-1929-3 (PB) • ISBN: 978-1-4711-1930-9 (eBook) • 10 9 8 7 6 5 4 3 2

On Sudden Hill

Linda Sarah and Benji Davies

SIMON AND SCHUSTER
London New York Sydney Toronto New Delhi

Two cardboard boxes,
big enough to sit in, hide inside.

Birt and Etho take them out each day,
climb up Sudden Hill and sit in them.

Sometimes they're kings,
soldiers, astronauts.
Sometimes they're pirates
sailing wild seas and skies.

But always, always
they're Big friends.

Their sailing, running, leaping, flying,
their chatter and giggles,
him and Etho,

their silences
and watching small movements
in the valley and feeling
big as Giant Kings.

Birt loves their two-by-two rhythm.

And then one Monday
(it's cramping cold)
they meet another box-carrier
who wants to join them.

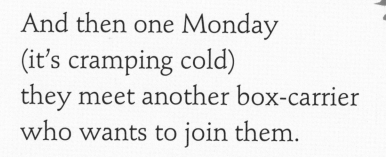

This tiny boy's called Shu.
He's watched Birt and Etho every day
and finally found a big enough box
and courage to ask if he can play too.

Etho smiles and says, "Sure!"
And so the three sit in their boxes,
watch one kestrel
and two lost clouds.

Sometimes they're dragon-slayers,
side-by-side house dwellers
and skyscraper dancers.

But Birt feels strange.

One night,
Birt smashes his box,
stamps on it,
rips it to bits.

His dad shouts something flat from the front room
about being quiet and that's enough!

Birt stops going up Sudden Hill.

Etho and Shu
call round sometimes.
Birt avoids them.

Instead he stays at home
mostly drawing pictures
of two boxes, side-by-side.

But he misses Etho.
He misses their cardboard
castles on Sudden Hill.

One day,
a knock on the door.

He hears Shu's voice.
"We made you something.
Please come out!"

All Birt can see
as he peeks
from the curtain
is a box.

But it's much,
much more
than a box.

It's got bright, waving things
attached to it like huge kites.
It's got colours.
It's got sound.
It's got, it's got – WHEELS!

The HUGE box-on-wheels
(that they call Mr ClimbFierce)
is hauled up Sudden Hill.

It's amazing!

An incredible Monster Creature Box Thing!

It's a supersonic rocket blaster!
A triple jet transformer!
A sparkling glitter king!

It's even got boxes inside,
one with biscuits, one with lemonade.

Birt likes Shu.
Shu is kind.
Shu is funny.
Shu is daring and brave.

Birt loves their time together,
their Etho-Shu-Birt-iness.

He loves their three-by-three rhythm.

It's new.
And it's good.